I0534303

A FIRE
IN THE
SHADOWS

A BOLINGBROOK BABBLER STORY
BOOK 1.5

WILLIAM BRINKMAN

Praise for the Bolingbrook Babbler Stories

Pathways to Bolingbrook:

"Two smart women trying to survive in difficult times. *Pathways to Bolingbrook* captures your imagination and leaves you wanting to know what happens next. Can't wait for the publication of the novel. Well worth reading." — Amazon reviewer.

"This is a very short introduction to what is sure to be an entertaining series, if just for ONE THING: Iowa is not boring." — Amazon reviewer.

"Keep reading. Keep writing, Mr. Brinkman, and all the best with your Anti-Psychic Kitty Press. Breathlessly waiting for your next publication. Six stars!" — Amazon reviewer.

A Fire in the Shadows:

"A thrilling 'vampire' fantasy packed full of twists, turns – and danger!" — Wishing Shelf.

"This was a fast-paced and exhilarating supernatural and sci-fi YA fantasy! The world-building and mythos that the author built into this series were evident immediately." — Author This was a fast-paced and exhilarating supernatural and sci-fi YA fantasy! The world-building and mythos that the author built into this series were evident immediately." — Anthony Avina, author

"I have never read a book so fast before! It sucks you in from the very first sentence. I can't wait to read more books from this author." — Goodreads reviewer.

The Rift:

"A richly written novel filled with memorable characters. Highly recommended!" — The Wishing Shelf.

"A quick, easy and interesting read that had good writing, a good storyline and well developed characters." — Goodreads reviewer.

"Every new development in the story surprised me and -- there are weredeer!I don't usually read fantasy or sci-fi, but this book made me want to take another look at the genre. I highly recommend it!" — Amazon reviewer.

"*The Rift* is a wild adventure, sprinkled with humor, duplicitous characters, and extraterrestrials. You never know who is working for the good of mankind or creating a rift in the world." — Amazon reviewer.

For the latest news about William Brinkman and the Bolingbrook Babbler stories, subscribe at https://bolingbrookbabbler.com/mailing-list

Copyright © 2023 by William Brinkman

All rights reserved.

No portion of this book may be reproduced in any form without written permission from the publisher or author, except as permitted by U.S. copyright law.

This book is entirely a work of fiction. Any institutions, businesses, or locations mentioned are either entirely fictional or used fictitiously. Any resemblance to actual persons, living or dead, or events is coincidental.

Book Cover by Miblart

First edition 2023

www.bolingbrookbabbler.com

For my wife, for being a bright light in the shadows.

A Fire in the Shadows

As Steve's blood warmed her body, Lydia recalled a memory from when she was a human named Miriam. Miriam was merely a high school student in Des Moines. Her new friend, Sheila, had invited her over as Miriam struggled in English, and Sheila offered to help. Miriam also hoped Sheila would teach her to twirl a baton, as Sheila was the baton twirler for the marching band. One of the best in the state. Miriam dreamed of becoming a baton twirler, but her father refused to pay for lessons — one of the countless requests he had denied.

Lydia could almost smell the potpourri in Sheila's room as she closed her eyes, remembering the vivid colors: the clean yellow walls, her pink leather appointment calendar, and posters of seemingly endless fields of flowers. Lydia's world faded as she lost herself in that joyous memory. She knew what awaited Miriam, but Lydia wanted to linger in the past for a while.

A hand patted Lydia's back. Startled, she sunk her fangs deeper into Steve's flesh. Steve tapped faster, his moaning a mixture of ecstasy and pain. Lydia retracted her fangs and licked the salty blood off his skin as Steve gently stroked her back. Lydia moved away. She felt relieved that the wound was healing, but also ashamed for accidentally hurting him.

She focused on the present as she sat in a booth at Barber's Corner Bar and Grill in Bolingbrook, Illinois. The customers reflected Bolingbrook's diverse population. People from different ethnic groups freely mingled with each other. A sharp contrast to Chicago's ethnic neighborhoods. Executives wearing suits sat at the bar with warehouse workers wearing t-shirts and work shorts.

Her companion, Steve, was the head of Bolingbrook's Department of Paranormal Affairs. The DPA was the Village of Bolingbrook's covert department tasked with concealing supernatural activities from Bolingbrook's residents and policing the local paranormal underworld. In theory, Lydia was one of the supernatural visitors the DPA was supposed to police. In practice, they just kept a cautious eye on her whenever she visited. Except for Steve. Over the years, their relationship evolved into a friendship. When she was with him, she felt alive.

Lydia noticed some patrons avoiding her gaze. They might have assumed Lydia was kissing Steve's neck. A few onlookers might have felt disgusted by their apparent age difference. Lydia looked like a white woman in her early to mid-20s with short dark brown hair, whilst Steve was a balding white male with graying remnants of hair left, and a scar etched on the right side of his face. He once told Lydia he was 25 years old, but Lydia suspected he was in his late 60s. He would never tell her how he got the scar. Lydia wondered if he would ever trust her with that secret. For now, he leaned into the corner of the bench as he caught his breath.

"Are you okay?" Lydia asked. "I'm sorry if—"

Steve shook his head, then placed both hands on the table to steady himself. "Don't apologize. It's my fault. I shouldn't have startled you."

"I'm just glad I didn't hurt you."

Steve sat up, then smiled at Lydia. "Quite the opposite. It felt good." Steve chuckled. "I guess I got nervous, and that's why I tapped. I should have said something, but you know how hard it is to talk."

Lydia relaxed. "I know."

Steve reached for his glass of orange juice. "So. Thank you, and I mean that. And please tell Marcus—"

"Matthew," Lydia corrected. "He's going by Matthew again."

"Matthew?" Steve carefully drank his juice.

Vampires that create new vampires are called blood parents. Matthew was her blood father, and she was his oldest blood daughter. Twenty years ago, he gave Miriam part of his vampiric essence. Over several days, Miriam faded away, until she died and was reborn as the vampire Lydia.

Lydia nodded. "He read a book last year and liked it so much, he adopted the author's first name."

Steve turned towards Lydia. "What book?" he asked, sounding intrigued.

"*The Skeptical Economy*? I think."

Steve's jaw dropped, and his glass almost slipped out of his hand. "You mean *The Skeptical Mind of the Economy*? By Professor Matthew Bennett?"

"Yeah. That's it."

Steve laughed as he turned towards the table and set down his glass. "Oh my God." He slapped the table a few times and stopped laughing. "I thought he'd be enthralled with Bennett. His whole thesis is that unregulated markets always result in ethical outcomes." Steve followed with another laughing fit. "He's always looking for a way to compensate for his psychopathy. I just didn't think he would rename himself Matthew."

"He didn't take his last name, if you're wondering."

"That would be too much for him." Steve placed his hands on the table and bowed his head. He took a couple of deep breaths, then sat up. He took another deep breath to calm himself. Steve sighed, then let out one last chuckle. "So," he finally said. "Is he still your CEO?"

"Yes, and we still operate as the Vitalis Corporation."

"Good. Because if he started calling himself the Knyaz—"

"Never."

In the vampire kingdoms, the leader takes the title of Knyaz. Matthew despised Knyaz and the whole vampiric monarchy. In the world of vampires, declaring yourself a CEO was akin to calling yourself an anarchist.

Steve drank most of his juice, then tipped his almost empty glass at Lydia. He smiled, but this time it was a polite smile. "Speaking of changes. Will Matthew be changing his terms?"

"No," Lydia replied. She felt disappointed that the conversation was shifting back to business matters.

Steve finished his juice, then swigged a glass of water. He almost slammed down the now empty glass. "Excellent. The village appreciates his generosity. Please let him know that."

"I will. The Vitalis Corporation appreciates the village's timely payments."

Steve sipped his water. "I also want to assure Matthew that my department is committed to protecting his investments from any unruly weredeer tourists."

Startled by him openly say the word "weredeer," Lydia looked for anyone eavesdropping. The patrons were watching the baseball games on the TVs above the bar or chatting with companions. To her surprise, no one seemed interested in a man talking about weredeer.

"Don't worry. Everyone talks about the *Babbler*, but nobody believes their stories."

Lydia chuckled at the mention of Bolingbrook's sensationalist tabloid. Most people in Bolingbrook didn't believe the *Babbler's* articles about the local shifters, or that Clow Airport was the public façade for the Earth's largest urban intergalactic spaceport. Lydia smirked. "You know we're long-time subscribers? They're one of Bolingbrook's more reliable newspapers."

Steve nodded. "You're right. I meant the people outside of the loop — my apologies."

Lydia's smile broadened. "Apology accepted."

"Unless there's anything else," said Steve, as he stood. "I should get going."

"I have a question."

Lydia's abdomen tensed, and her heart started beating. Steve was her only human companion. She worried her question could end their friendship

Steve sat back down and waited a moment. "Go on."

Lydia's body tensed. "What about the residents?"

Steve gave her a quizzical look. "The residents?" he asked.

"Will you be protecting them as well?" she asked with a pained voice.

Steve furrowed his brow, then spent a few seconds intensely studying Lydia with his eyes. His gaze unsettled Lydia. He cleared his throat, ending the silence. "We'll do our job."

"Do your job?" Despite her anxiety, she couldn't accept his evasive answer.

"Is that a problem?" he asked in a matter-of-fact tone.

Steve's stoic face unnerved Lydia. She took a few moments to consider her words. "It—"

She paused as a chill rippled through her; she had fought and faced creatures far deadlier than Steve. Yet she feared his reaction the most. However, she still needed to know his answer.

"Steve." Lydia continued, "You're a protector. It's why I admire you. Yet..." She paused, then took a deep breath. "Sometimes you seem to value institutions over people.

Maybe you think you're serving a higher cause or fighting for the greater good." Steve shifted awkwardly at her words, but she persisted. "I worry you might sacrifice the residents for what you believe is a higher cause. Like, say, protecting our investments."

"I gave Matthew my word that I would," Steve replied.

"I know." Lydia worked up the courage to continue. "So, I want to remind you we consider Bolingbrook's residents one of our investments. Not as blood bags, but as people." Lydia flashed a smile, pressing her teeth against her lower lip. "They're worth defending, too. I hope you understand."

Steve remained silent for what seemed to Lydia like several uncomfortable moments. Lifting an empty glass, he pretended to take a swig, and tapped his index finger against the rim five times. Four white males who were sitting in different areas of the bar, simultaneously stood up. Except for their uniform crew cuts, they were indistinguishable from the other patrons. Each one carried a concealed weapon. They exited the bar. Steve waited until the last one left. "Before I answer your questions, I'll need to explain the situation. I trust you won't tell the *Babbler*?"

"Agreed," she replied, not expecting this response from Steve.

"After that," he said, then paused. "I hope you will answer my question."

Lydia nodded, though unsure of what his question would be.

Steve paused, as if to weigh what he was about to say. "Now, you're being a bit unfair. I don't always value institutions over people. Just between you and me, I think there are institutions that should be destroyed for the greater good. Likewise, there are people who *should* be killed for the greater good."

Lydia masked her disappointment at his words. She expected better from him than this equivocation. Lydia knew he could act like a politician, but they weren't talking about garbage toters, or property taxes. They were talking about an army of misogynistic predators gathering near Bolingbrook.

Steve continued. "I bring this up so I can explain why the weredeer are gathering here. You can say they're mercenaries hired as backup."

"Backup?" Lydia moved her head back for a moment. "For whom?"

Steve shifted uncomfortably on the bench and looked down at the table. "It's complicated." He tapped his fingers on the table, then faced Lydia. "There is an ongoing conflict within a very important institution. You wouldn't recognize the name. Both sides are coming here — one side inside of the Bolingbrook Golf Club and the other protesting outside. The weredeer will back up the protestors."

Lydia blinked. "How?" She'd never heard of weredeer working as mercenaries.

"They say they have plans to end the conflict," Steve answered. "I know very little about their Plan A, and I don't want to know, to be honest. The weredeer are for their Plan B." Steve tilted his head for a moment. "They've assured me," he added, "That both plans will have minimal spillover into the community."

"Minimal?" Lydia asked, perplexed by his answer. She'd never heard of any weredeer with the ability to show restraint. Especially if they were in their alpha deer form. Even with the DPA's considerable resources, she doubted their ability to contain an army of raging weredeer. "Why not prevent it instead?"

Steve averted his eyes from Lydia. "For reasons I cannot discuss, but if their little conflict gets out of hand, we'll protect Bolingbrook." He faced Lydia. "And its residents. You have my word, and you know I can back it up. This goes beyond the weredeer threat as well." He gave Lydia a forced smile. "Does that answer your question?"

"Yes, but I hope you can find a peaceful end to this." Otherwise, it wouldn't end well, she thought.

Steve shrugged. "If the opportunity presents itself, I will."

Lydia tried to hide her disappointment. "Good to hear." Part of her wanted to press Steve for a better answer. Another part of her wanted to cling to her only human friend.

Steve looked around the bar. "Now, before I ask my question, I need to know if Aurora or any of your co-workers are here."

Only her younger blood sister, Aurora, accompanied her to Bolingbrook. Aurora was supposed to be meeting her contacts tonight. Matthew and the rest were staying in the Quad Cities.

"I'm the only one." Lydia was worried he was going to ask her to keep a secret from her blood family and her coworkers. She couldn't betray their trust, but she also didn't want to lose Steve.

"Very well." Steve paused. "When did it start?"

She raised an eyebrow. "Start?"

Steve shifted closer to Lydia. "Most vampires don't apologize and, if they do, they're being sarcastic. They also can't stop talking about themselves." He paused, then took a deep breath. "Now, you've made some sarcastic remarks over the years, but you're not selfish. You never have been."

Lydia tensed. She didn't hide her feelings from him. Yet, knowing that he was aware of them made her feel embarrassed and vulnerable.

Steve continued. "I don't pretend to know everything about vampires and, honestly, I don't want to. I know vampires lose the ability to feel empathy, love, kindness, and even compassion. Someone from one of Chicago's courts explained it to me. She said becoming a vampire is like setting your soul on fire." He focused on Lydia's face as he continued. "A vampire fuels that fire with blood and harnesses the flames to gain power and eternal renewal. But that same fire consumes what she called 'soft emoti ons.'"

"You've met the Counselor?" asked Lydia. The Counselor was the oldest vampire in Chicago. Someone Lydia had the good fortune of never meeting. Matthew, however, knew her, and could spend an entire night ranting about her. Based on his descriptions of the Counselor, 'soft emotions' sounded like something she would say.

Steve nodded. "I know about her rivalry with Matthew; I would never betray Matthew — or you — to her. One of the best ways to protect your investment is to not make her angry." He paused, surveying Lydia closely. "So, when did you start having feelings again?"

She froze, feeling her heart thunder against her chest as she studied Steve for any signs of deception.

"You don't have to answer." He added sympathetically.

Lydia glanced around the bar. None of the patrons seemed to care. They must have found the White Sox game more interesting. "I don't know." She looked up for a moment. "Maybe it was five years ago. Maybe longer. It was so gradual at first; at some point, I knew I wasn't the same. I was different." Lydia had lost fights in the past, but she never felt as vulnerable as she did now.

Steve reached towards Lydia's hand, clasping his warm fingers around hers. She put her other hand on top of his and smiled. How long, she wondered, had it been since she'd felt someone's affectionate touch? She hoped it was a sign that they have a future together. Steve returned her smile for a moment. He continued. "The older ones kill those they suspect of having your condition. Is that correct?"

"Yes," she whispered.

"And Matthew knows?"

"They know." Lydia looked down at Steve's hand. "They figured it out."

"Have they harmed you?"

Lydia shook her head and faced Steve. "No. They tease me, but that's all they do. We... We still protect each other."

"They protect you, but they don't understand you. Right?"

Lydia tried to speak, but her throat tightened. Steve was right. He was the first person since her rebirth that could articulate how she felt.

"I can see your answer." Steve flashed a sympathetic smile. "It makes sense. Matthew wants to be different, but he still can't feel emotions like you can." Steve used his free hand to pat Lydia's arm. "While humans have those emotions, many would see you as a monster. It must be hard. You're surrounded by vampires and humans, yet you must feel so alone."

Lydia nodded in agreement. "I do." She replied with a hint of nervousness in her voice.

Steve averted his eyes from her gaze, loosening his grasp and removing his other hand. Lydia cautiously withdrew her free hand. Steve focused on their clasped hands. He drew a quick breath. "You might wonder if I'm someone who can give you the love you so desperately want. Maybe you're worried our relationship is purely transactional. It's more than that, but —" Steve tightened his grip. Instead of the leader of the Department of Paranormal Affairs, Lydia was with a desperate man struggling to retain control. "You're a good person. I wish there were more vampires like you. Hell, I wish there were more humans like you." Steve released her hand. "You should be with a good person. I'm not one, but I would be a terrible person if I didn't tell you the truth."

"But—"

"Lydia," he interrupted. "I can't give you what you need. What you want. What you deserve." He rubbed his eyes for a moment. "I sincerely hope you find someone who can."

Lydia spun away from Steve, intently facing the wall. She didn't want him to see her in pain. Losing her emotional connection with Steve was upsetting. Lydia also felt ashamed for thinking it was possible to have any kind of relationship with Steve. Why, she wondered, did she think a bureaucrat could ever love her?

"I hope we can—"

"Goodbye," Lydia snapped. "Matthew will call."

Steve sighed. He removed some cash from his wallet and placed it on the table. "It's on me." He sniffled as he pretended to adjust his tie. "We will do our best to protect Bolingbrook. I promise."

Lydia's only recognition of his words was a slight nod of her head.

"Goodbye, Lydia." Steve left the booth.

She felt her body go numb as she beheld the dirty dollar bills he had discarded on the table; it reminded her of all the people who had paid before disposing of her too. As if a wad of cash could make it okay. Lydia fought the urge to smash the table. She'd known Steve for nearly 20 years. At first, their meetings involved discussing business matters, followed by Steve offering his blood to her. Later, Lydia felt affectionate towards Steve. That was also when their meetings felt more like dates. Sometimes, whenever a vampire teased her, she imagined having a future with Steve. He'd just shattered that dream.

Lydia started to stand when she heard Sara Langston — an African American woman in her thirties — placing an order with a waitress. Sara wore a dark red blouse that complimented her complexion. The ceiling lights glimmered off her silver ear studs. Despite the excitement in the air, she remained calm and collected.

Lydia knew Sara was the editor of the *Babbler*. She had only seen her a few times since arriving in Bolingbrook. Yet something about Sara always drew Lydia's attention. She sat down and watched Sara.

Across from Sara sat an African American woman in her early 20s. She fidgeted as she looked at her full glass of beer. Sara placed her hands on the table and clasped her hands. "Now," said Sara. "In this bar, I'm not the editor. I'm Sara. You're not a probationary reporter. You're someone I know. We're not in the newsroom. We're not on assignment."

The woman looked up from her drink. "So?"

"So... this is between us." Sara smiled. "Now, what's going on?"

"I don't know if I'm cut out for this," she replied, sounding defeated

"I ran your last article," Sara countered. "And you know I don't print subpar stories."

"Thank you. I guess I'm just frustrated with my 'girls in green' investigation. Nothing but dead ends. Don thinks I'm wasting my time, and the others agree. I can write, but..."

Lydia sympathized with the young reporter. The girls in green were a mystery to Lydia and to most of the paranormal residents of Bolingbrook. Their ability to disguise their appearance was unrivaled. Even with her heightened senses, Lydia might have only caught a glance at one of them. Matthew believed they were genetically engineered spies. Perhaps they complimented the village's enforcers, the men in blue. Others speculated they were fae. Those who knew either weren't talking or weren't alive.

"But?" asked Sara.

"I saw one when I was a kid. I was looking for my lost library book because if I didn't, my parents would have to pay a fine. Then a woman wearing a green outfit handed it to me. Then she vanished. Just like that." The woman snapped her fingers. "It's bothered me ever since. I thought if I joined the *Babbler*, I could learn more about them. Instead, I only have more questions."

"You're not alone. Many reporters have tried. Even Don. I heard he investigated them for ten years before giving up. I imagine Don and the others don't want you to be frustrated."

"Do you think I should give up?"

Sara shifted her lips, as if she was considering her response. Lydia and the woman anxiously awaited Sara's reply. "More like take a break," said Sara with a supportive tone. "You know how a watched kettle never boils?"

She nodded.

"Same with the girls in green. If you look for them, you won't find them — they'll find you. They've revealed themselves to you once. There's a good chance you'll see them again."

"Really?"

"Really. Until then, focus on other things. Believe it or not, there's more to Bolingbrook than aliens and were-deer."

Lydia kept listening to Sara's soothing voice, and the honesty shared with her companion. Lydia had enough experience using her heightened senses to determine when a human was lying. Contrary to the myths, vampires don't have the power to read or control minds. Instead, vampires can communicate telepathically with another. They call it *whispering*.

Aw. Did he hurt you? Should your little sister kiss your booboo and make it all better?

Lydia sighed as Aurora, a woman of east Asian ancestry, strolled into the bar. She was shorter than Lydia and had short black hair. Her brown eyes focused on Lydia as she strolled towards the booth. Aurora's black leather motorcycle jacket stood out in contrast to everyone else's casual attire. Aurora picked up two empty beer bottles as she approached, and Lydia gestured pointedly to the other side of the table. Nudging Lydia, Aurora sat beside her, setting a bottle down as Lydia shifted away.

Thirsty?

I'm fine.

Aurora pretended to be shocked.

Lydia! How are we supposed to sell our animal blood if you're drinking the blood of humans? Not a good look for a Vitalis employee. Don't you think?

Two things. First, I've lost count of the number of vials I've drunk. Second, we're allowed to drink from willing donors. You know our product is an alternative to hunting people. It would only look bad if I chose hunting over drinking.

Aurora pulled out a dark plastic vial and poured its contents into her beer bottle. The dark red fluid flowed out of the vial like whole milk poured from a carton. If she wasn't full, Lydia would have accepted Aurora's offer. The blood Vitalis sold was just as good as human blood. Though drinking the blood of a willing human donor felt more intimate to Lydia. Giving a donor a feeding high while savoring that donor's blood was like sex with a loving partner. In those all too brief moments, Lydia didn't feel alone.

Aurora whispered. *Well. Tonight, I guess it's up to me to promote it.*

Aurora drank what smelled like a mix of stale beer and blood. She gave Lydia an exaggerated smile.

All the blood. None of the hassles! That should be our slogan.

Matthew created the Vitalis Corporation to sell animal blood to the vampires in the Great Lakes region. Collecting blood from the slaughterhouses in Iowa and Illinois, they filtered out the impurities and distributed the vials to their customers; it was a profitable market. Vampires who hunted humans for blood risked drawing the attention of either covert government agencies or freelance monster hunters. Vitalis sold a convenient, safe supply of easy blood. All the blood. None of the hassles.

Lydia appreciated Vitalis didn't slaughter animals specifically to get their blood. The meat industry had already condemned them to death. When she couldn't disassociate herself while watching knockers kill cattle, she started working on more humane alternatives. Despite her efforts, Lydia had yet to create a business plan that satisfied Matthew.

Vitalis was only an element of Matthew's greater plan; he wanted to change the world so vampires could openly and peacefully co-exist with humans. He believed such an arrangement would benefit both parties. Most Vitalis customers, however, just wanted a safe source of blood.

Other vampires felt threatened by Matthew's vision or wanted to monopolize the animal blood market. Among vampires, violence and last death were acceptable business tactics. Because of this, the employees of Vitalis needed to work together to survive. Working for the corporation helped Lydia survive as a vampire. Being Matthew's blood daughter helped her standing within the company. But Lydia's employment wasn't based on nepotism. She excelled at reconnaissance. Based on the conversations she overheard, she might be one of the best scouts in Vitalis' history.

Aurora finished her bottle and licked her lips clean.

"Find anyone?" asked Lydia.

Aurora stopped smirking. "Kind of. The domesticated deer shifters are running away or hiding. I caught Lucy before she left."

"Lucy left Bolingbrook?" asked Lydia in disbelief. Lucy was a weredeer who lived in Bolingbrook with her human husband. She was also a reliable source regarding Bolingbrook's other paranormal residents. She couldn't imagine her running away from the village she had deep connections with.

"I know," Aurora replied. "She says it's the largest army of feral weredeer she's ever seen, and it's still growing. Apparently, the ferals hate domesticated weredeer. Lucy doesn't think they're here to kill her kind, but she doesn't want to risk it."

Lydia nodded. "Steve said that they're mercenaries for some battle that's going to happen at the Bolingbrook Golf Club."

"That white elephant? Seriously?"

"Seriously. He assured me the department would defend Bolingbrook while they fight it out. That's all I got from him."

Aurora gave Lydia a skeptical look. "Was he telling the truth?"

"Yes. He knows what will happen if they devastate Bolingbrook. If the New World Order — or what's left of the Illuminati — don't kill him, Matthew will. After our CSO had his way with him."

Aurora giggled. "I'd love to see that. I wonder if I should—"

"Shut up," Lydia protested. "You're morbid, even for a vampire." Lydia regretted mentioning the Corporate Security Officer.

"Oh, lighten up, Lydia. I just think it's funny to imagine Steve begging—"

Lydia growled, "What part of 'shut up' don't you understand?"

Startled, Aurora moved her head back for a moment. She examined Lydia with her curious eyes. After a few moments, she shrugged and relaxed. "Fine. I just see the humor in Steve being tortured after torturing so many others."

Lydia locked eyes with Aurora. Lydia wondered why Aurora had to remind her. She'd heard rumors of Steve electrocuting shifters and waterboarding occultists. She hated that part of him. Because Aurora reminded her, she felt worse for having feelings for Steve.

Aurora giggled. "Chill out. We're blood sisters, remember? You can't hate your sister."

"I don't hate you," Lydia retorted as she lowered her eyes. "You're just annoying."

Aurora pretended to be wounded, placing both hands theatrically over her heart before falling backwards as Lydia shook her head. She wondered if Miriam was ever this annoying to her older sister. Yet Lydia also felt a bond with Aurora. Aurora could be cruel, but she would stick by her side.

Aurora sprung back into a seated position. "So? You never answered my question: did he make you cry?"

Lydia side-eyed her sister. "Fuck you."

"I'm your sister, remember?"

"Don't remind me."

"So, did he? Did he make you cry? Did you make tears? Vampires can't shed tears, but I bet you did. Tell me if they were tears of blood or saltwater. I bet it was blood. Was it? Did you really waste blood on him, Lydia?"

Aurora kept talking, but Lydia focused on Sara and her companion, using her heightened sight and hearing. Both women were more interested in their conversation than their drinks.

"I think you should take over the weredeer story," said Sara.

"Me? I thought you assigned a freelance reporter."

"We lost touch with him. I don't think he ran away, and Wendy is still trying to figure out what happened. If he's still alive, we'll help him. But for now, we need someone to cover the story, and I would like you to take over."

"Okay, but it sounds dangerous."

"Not if we take a different approach. I'll give you the list of eyewitnesses to interview and you don't have to worry about getting photos. We'll use file photos instead. So that should minimize the risk."

Aurora stopped talking and frowned. She looked towards Sara's booth. "You know them?"

"The woman on the left is Sara. She's the *Babbler's* editor now. Not sure about the other woman."

"So, *that's* Sara."

"Yes. I saw her on my first patrol."

Aurora studied Lydia's face, then looked at Sara. "Are you rebounding already?" Lydia's focus remained solely on Sara as Aurora gave her the side-eye. "She's a bit too old to twilight, don't you think?" asked Aurora.

"Twilighting" was when a vampire pretended to be in love with a young person as a joke. The *Twilight* series inspired both the fad and the term.

Lydia glared at her sister, who merely shrugged in response.

"It's true," Aurora replied. "She looks too old. The one on the right is a better target."

"Target? Really, Aurora?"

"Okay. Why Sara then?"

Lydia shook her head, then returned her attention to Sara once more. She was telling a story about a rare book collector she met in Chicago. Lydia kept her focus on Sara. "You wouldn't understand."

"Let me guess, then." Aurora squinted at Sara for a moment. "Is it the hair? You just want to reach out and touch it? Is it her nails? Her boobs? Her chocolate—"

"She's not food," snapped Lydia.

"You're right. We would drink her blood, not eat her. Good point."

Lydia snarled. "Drop it, Aurora."

"After you explain why you want to twilight an adult."

Lydia sighed. "I don't want to twilight her. You wouldn't understand."

"Try me."

Lydia looked back at Sara. She found some people's faces alluring, but could never articulate the characteristics she desired. Lydia felt that desire when she looked at Sara's face. But it wasn't just physical attraction. The way Sara cared about her companion brought back memories from her childhood. When their father was in his study, Miriam and her sister would spend time with their cats. Her sister taught Miriam about feline care, like the right way to hold a cat, and the best games to play with them. In those moments, her caring voice warmed Miriam's heart and helped her feel safe. Just like Sara's voice was making her feel. "She feels like... home."

Aurora gave Lydia a quizzical look. "Home?" She squinted as she scanned Sara, as if she was trying to see what Lydia was seeing.

"I said you wouldn't understand."

Lydia shifted her focus back to Sara. Home is the right word, she thought.

Aurora observed Lydia for a few moments before clearing her throat. "I hate to interrupt your uncomfortable staring, but I still haven't heard from Vlad or any of the Reds. We should find them."

Lydia watched Sara for a few beats. "You're right." Lydia sighed.

Aurora smirked. "One of us has to be the blood sibling."

Collecting her jacket, Lydia pretended not to hear her blood sister as she moved to leave. Sara looked in Lydia's direction, only briefly, yet Lydia averted her gaze and left the bar, crossing over to the parking lot. She wondered if she was rebounding. No, Lydia thought. She felt the attraction before tonight. It had to be more than Steve.

Aurora broke the silence. "Really, Lydia? Another human? You have way too much blood in your fire."

"Fuck you."

"Our plumbing doesn't work. Remember?" Aurora giggled. Lydia didn't reply to Aurora's dirty joke. After their rebirth, vampires lose the ability to have orgasms. For vampires with blood in their fire, love and attraction are purely emotional experiences.

Aurora smirked. "I hope you didn't spend the last three nights swooning over Steve or her."

"No. Did you spend the last three nights with the Night Flyers?"

"No. You know, that's different." The Night Flyers were one of the vampire gangs contracted to guard Bolingbrook on Vitalis' behalf. Lydia felt they were better party organizers than fighters. "Seriously, Lydia — what do you see in her? Do you think she will understand you?"

"She might."

"Because you think she's hot?"

"Because I could be myself with her. She already knows about vampires."

Aurora shook her head. "She knows more than the average person, but is that enough? Let's set aside the whole immortality thing. What kind of relationship could you have with her? Do you think she'll wait for you while we're traveling? What will your conversations be like and what if your past comes up? You didn't always have blood in your fire. Remember all the fun things we used to do?"

Aurora's words stung. When she was a new vampire, Lydia was just as sadistic as Aurora. At one point, they were called the terror sisters. Since she regained her empathy, Lydia felt ashamed of who she was.

Aurora pressed on. "How would you handle the whole day and night schedules? She'll wake up just as you're about to sleep. Are you two going to say 'Shalom Shabbat' to each other? Or is it Shabbat Shalom? Ooh — I just thought of this! Before you drink her blood, what will you say?" Aurora said *L'chaim* like she was coughing up phlegm while laughing. "That's not right. What's the Hebrew word for 'Un-life?'"

Rage burned within Lydia. Growing up, her father never invested in her Jewish instruction. She, along with her father, never kept kosher and never observed the Sabbath. He never paid for her to go to Sunday School. Her sister taught her some Hebrew when their father wasn't around. Yet, some people still bullied Miriam because of her Ashkenazi heritage. A heritage she felt little connection to. Choosing the Greek name Lydia as her rebirth name was her way to sever that connection and start anew. Aurora knew that mentioning anything related to Judaism bothered Lydia.

"I don't know," Lydia growled. "What's Mandarin for 'shut up?'" Aurora also hated any mention of her mortal heritage. Lydia hoped her quip would silence Aurora.

Instead, Aurora firmly grabbed Lydia's arm, pulling her body close. They locked gazes as Aurora's fangs bared for a moment. "Let me set you straight, sister. I am a vampire." Her grip tightened. "That woman is dead. I emerged from the flames of her soul. So don't you—"

Aurora's grip loosened as her eyes averted to Lydia's side.

Fuck.

What?

There's a Cerza behind you.

Cerza was slang for Rycerz. They were the enforcers, or 'knights' from the Kingdom of Northern Chicago. Aurora telepathically projected what she saw; across Boughton Road, a white male vampire, seemingly in his early 20s, stood on the roof of Portillo's. He was looking in their direction. The faint purple paint splotches on his black jacket marked him as a Cerza.

Lydia replied: *One knife. Not blending with the shadows. Newbie.*

Agreed. Walk away. I'll distract him. You get behind him.

Cool. This is the Lydia I like.

Aurora stepped back, pretending to be shocked. "You bitch!"

Lydia backed away and raised her hands. "Better a bitch than a blood ember!"

Blood ember?

He'll think you're too weak to worry about.

Aurora grinned. *He'll be in for a surprise.*

Aurora flipped Lydia off and walked away. Lydia slapped the nearest car; the alarm ripped throughout Barber's Corner. "Oh, shut up!" Lydia bellowed, pretending to be angry. Lydia approached her motorcycle, hoping the Cerza's focus was on her. When she reached her motorcycle, she positioned herself and blocked the view of the side cases. Putting on her jacket, she grasped the combat knife from her side case and placed it in her interior pocket, hoping the Cerza couldn't see it.

Wooden stakes were worthless against vampires. Matthew proved this once by stabbing himself with one. It shattered as soon as it struck his sternum. The right combat knife, he said, could dust a vampire's limbs. Lydia hoped it wouldn't come to that. It took several days for most vampires to heal a severed limb; sometimes it was kinder to end a fight with a bone breaking punch.

Aurora projected her point of view as she landed on the roof. The surprised Cerza turned and froze. Aurora hissed at him. He bared his fangs and charged.

Your turn, sis.

Lydia closed the case, then stepped away from the street-lamps lighting the parking lot. Blending into the shadows, she rendered herself invisible to mortals and the younger generation of vampires. When she was Miriam, Matthew had showed this to her; she recollected her shock as darkness enveloped her body. Now she could do that and see through the darkness.

Lydia jumped, generating a telekinetic "push" to propel her into the night sky. She couldn't fly like Matthew or the older vampires, but she could leap at least a quarter of a mile high, twisting midair like a gymnast.

Below her, the Cerza scout displayed his inexperience by throwing wild punches and off-balance kicks. Aurora feigned fear as she toyed with him. Her quick and powerful strikes hinting at her experience. Lydia landed on the scout, knocking him down as she tugged him into a restraint. He struggled yet couldn't break free. Lydia pulled the scout to his feet as he continued writhing. Aurora squeezed his throat.

"Be quiet," ordered Aurora, "Unless you want me to dust your eyes. Got it?" The scout nodded and Aurora grinned. "Better."

Her grip loosened.

"You can't do—"

Aurora silenced him by squeezing harder. "I said *quiet*. Do you want to end up in a DPA cell? They aren't as friendly as the Orange Squad."

The scout's eyes widened. The Orange Squad was the nickname of the mortal group that policed Chicago's supernatural residents. Not even Matthew knew if they were a covert division of the Chicago Police Department, or a group of well-connected contractors. Regardless of their origin, no one disputed their ruthlessness.

Aurora smirked. "Now. Let's try this again." She released her grip but, a moment later, smacked the scout across his face. "Use your voice so my blood sister can hear you."

"How dare you." He said in a stage whisper. The fear in his eyes betrayed his bravado act. Definitely a recruit, Lydia thought.

"Good." Aurora whispered back. "Don't talk any louder than that."

"Don't you know who I am?" The Cerza replied with anger and contempt in his voice. "I'm a Rycerz of the Chicago Kingdom."

Aurora laughed. "Someone's claimed all of Chicago."

Lydia snorted.

"You might want to tell that to the Lincoln Dominion, the Chiraq Union, the Western Kingdom, and —" Aurora looked at Lydia. "—how many other Chicago territories?"

"Ten." Lydia replied.

"Your dude hosts a human role-playing game every week. I can't see him conquering Chicago. Even with his lucky dice, he'd struggle to capture an office with a view." Aurora smirked. "They look so cute when they pretend to be humans."

The scout struggled and bared his fangs. "You'll answer for that."

"Please," pleaded Lydia. "Just tell us why you're here and who came with you. Then you can go home."

"A Rycerz does not answer questions from bandits," he replied. He sounded indignant, but Lydia also sensed fear in his voice.

"Seriously?" Lydia snapped.

Aurora shook her head. "You must really love your dude if—"

"I serve the Dux," he said with a now shaky voice. "You will pay for mocking the rightful ruler of Chicago." Lydia wondered if he was threatening them or trying to reassure himself.

Aurora giggled. "That wasn't mockery. This is." Aurora pretended to hold a scepter and pointed her nose at the sky. She began performing an exaggerated high step march. Using her worst imitation of a male voice, she said, "I am the High Dude of Chicago. The great pretender. Heir of hair." Aurora stopped pretending and walked up to him. She leaned in, almost touching his forehead. "That, Mr. Paladin, is mockery."

The scout attempted to break Lydia's grasp.

"Stop it," Lydia hissed. "Just tell us why you're here."

"And who are you with?" Aurora asked. "Enforcers always travel outside of Chicago in a posse."

The scout stopped struggling but looked away from the pair.

"I think we might have to loosen his tongue," said Aurora.

Lydia whispered in the scout's ear, "It's not worth it. Just talk."

The scout chuckled. "You're playing good cop, bad cop," he replied in a more confident tone.

"Not really," Aurora replied. "She's the good cop." Aurora kicked his groin, the blow lifting him several inches as the crack of his hips resounded. Lydia winced as the scout collapsed; she tried to lift him. Aurora grabbed his throat and pulled him up. Aurora said, "I'm the kind of bad cop." The scout struggled to stand. "That really hurt. Right?" Aurora sneered, pressing her fingernails into his skin. "Right?" The scout struggled to nod as he looked at Aurora in agony. Aurora grinned. "That's nothing compared to what our CSO can do. He knows all the spots. You won't die, but you'll wish you were dead. Just ask my blood sister. She used to love his work."

"Yes," Lydia replied, ashamed of the times she used to cheer him on as he made the toughest vampires beg for mercy. When he worked over mortal vampire hunters, Aurora and she would play torture bingo.

Aurora continued. "Now, you have a choice. Answer our questions or meet our CSO."

Aurora released his throat. He groaned in agony as he struggled to stand. The scout closed his eyes and took short, labored breaths. Aurora's face beamed with joy as she watched. Lydia heard his bones slowly healing.

"Fine," he moaned. The scout took a few more labored breaths. "We're investigating the weredeer intrusion."

Aurora's eyes sparkled with pride. "How many is we?"

"Five."

"Including you?"

"Yes."

Aurora's eyes widened as she glanced at Lydia. Lydia thought sending five Cerzas into Bolingbrook was a brazen move by the Dux. The court knew how to reach Matthew to request permission. She wondered if they were using the weredeer army's arrival as pretext to seize Bolingbrook.

"Finally," Aurora excitedly replied. "We're getting somewhere. What have you learned?"

"The one we captured said he was following the plan. That's all we got before we released him. The Red Raiders told us the weredeer are waiting for orders."

"You spoke to the Reds?" Aurora asked.

"The ones we spared talked." He smiled pridefully at Aurora. His hips healed enough for him to stand on his own.

The Reds were the other gang guarding Bolingbrook. Lydia felt they were the most responsible of the two gangs.

"That sucks," Aurora casually replied. "They were fun, and you broke them."

The scout straightened his posture and cast an angry gaze at Aurora. "They defied the rightful Dux of Chicago."

Lydia tightened her hold in response to his callous attitude. "Bolingbrook isn't part of your kingdom. You had no right to do that." She bared her fangs and pulled his head by the hair. "You want to join them?"

Easy, sister. Aurora shot a warning glare at Lydia. Lydia nodded. She retracted her fangs and released his head.

"So," Aurora asked. "Where are your friends?"

The scout tried to stick his chest out. "We are the—"

Aurora kicked his knee, hyper-extending it. The scout screamed as he dropped to his good knee. Aurora reached for this throat, but he closed his mouth and struggled to contain his anguished cries. Lydia forced him to lie on his stomach, then put her weight on his back. Pinned to the floor, the scout looked up at Aurora.

"Where are they?" asked Aurora.

He took a few shallow breaths before he could speak. "They're waiting for the editor."

"Editor?" asked Lydia, but she knew there was only one editor to ask regarding paranormal activity in Bolingbrook.

"*The Babbler's.*"

Lydia froze. Her heart pounded inside her chest.

Aurora chuckled. "You're in Bolingbrook. Buy a copy."

"She might know more than they've printed."

Lydia shook her head, "No, she knows less than you do. Leave her alone."

"Too late."

Lydia tried to filter out the traffic sounds from Boughton Road and Route 53. When she finally heard a car engine starting, she looked back towards Barber's Corner. Lydia spotted Sara in her white sedan as she drove from the parking lot; a male Cerza on a motorcycle followed, as did a black car.

"Call them off," snapped Lydia.

The scout shook his head. "I don't have the authority."

"Ask."

"Why?" he replied with a smirk.

"Wrong answer." Lydia wrenched both his arms back. Aurora gasped as Lydia dislocated the scout's shoulders. He let out an unrestrained scream as his shoulder muscles spasmed. Lydia slammed his head into the floor twice. Aurora's eyes widened.

"Lydia?" she asked with alarm in her voice.

The scout gasped for air, which Lydia believed was his instinctive response to the extreme pain.

Lydia looked up at Aurora. *After he heals, get him a ride home.*

Lydia jumped to her feet. The scout didn't move; His face seemed frozen with a shocked expression.

What are you doing, Lydia?

Protecting Sara.

They'll kill you!

They'll try.

Sara turned, driving south along Bolingbrook Drive as the Cerza followed. Lydia propelled herself towards the sky, blending with the darkness as she sensed a whisper from Aurora.

She's not worth it!

Lydia leaped over Boughton Road, landed past the Taco Bell on Bolingbrook Drive, and sprinted south. Vampires could run up to 70 miles per hour. Much faster than the cars beside her.

Lydia remembered the first time she saw Sara, catching her eye from the moment she stepped out of her cubicle. She didn't manage her colleagues through intimidation — no; she was kind, but firm when she needed to be. Lydia specifically remembered hearing Sara talking to Wendy, the graphic designer and unofficial paranormal expert, about a freelance writer. Perhaps the same one Sara mentioned in the bar; Sara believed something had happened to him, and she wasn't giving up until she found out what. Sara's caring nature was one reason Lydia found attractive. Lydia started feeling more confident about her feelings for Sara. It wasn't a rebound or infatuation. Sara was right for her, and better for her than Steve could have ever been.

Lydia slowed as she approached the pursuing Cerza. Traffic backed up at the stoplight; Lydia couldn't risk confronting them there. A public brawl wasn't the best way to introduce vampires to humanity.

Matthew had been teaching her a shadow blending technique that worked in lighted areas. The patterns disturbed humans so they would subconsciously look away. This would be her first unsupervised attempt. It was a risk, but then she pictured the scout terrorizing Sara; the risk was worth it.

Lydia hopped on top of a box truck and lied prone, sliding across the roof. No one could see her. Vampires were immune to this kind of shadow blending, so she had to act carefully.

On the other side was the Cerza's car and motorcycle driver; two white males were in the car, both with Cerza markings on their jackets. The passenger sat in the backseat while she discerned the zip ties from his jacket pocket.

The light changed to green. Lydia clenched the edge of the roof as the truck moved forward, then spotted the motorcycle driver. Lydia could tell he was skilled at following cars without being noticed. She'd done it herself in the past.

Lydia scanned the area, and even the night sky. She didn't see the fifth Cerza. Where was he?

Lydia shuddered at the thought of the fifth one waiting at Sara's place. No, they wouldn't be following her, she thought. They'd be waiting there for her.

Instead, Lydia suspected the motorcycle guy was going to get ahead of Sara, forcing her to stop. The car would park behind her while they tugged her from the car and into theirs. A classic block and grab, Lydia thought.

In the car, the passenger kept looking out the window onto ground level. Lydia guessed the scout had warned them, but the passenger didn't know how to spot vampire tails.

Amateurs, thought Lydia.

Sara turned left onto Briarcliff Road, the motorcycle and car continuing to follow. Lydia leaped off the truck and over a strip mall. She landed on the roof of an apartment and pursued the Cerzas.

Lydia imagined the Cerzas as one giant snake threatening Sara. How, she wondered, should she attack the snake? Cut off the head or slash the body?

Lydia hopped from rooftop to rooftop as she tailed them. The Cerzas seemed hyper focused on Sara as the traffic thinned; Sara and the Cerzas drove further down Briarcliff. When the last bystander flashed their turn signal, the motorcycle closed in on Sara. The bystander turned on to Annerino Drive, and the Cerza's car secured the distance.

Slash the body, thought Lydia. They need a car to move Sara. No car. No kidnapping.

Lydia leaped off a rooftop and propelled herself at the Cerza's car. She slammed her shoulder into the driver's side door, leaving a sizable dent. Before the driver could recover, the car jumped the curb. It crashed into a tree at the top of the embankment as Lydia rolled to her feet and charged at the car. The front of the car resembled a crushed can. Lydia's impact left a crater-like dent in the driver's side door. The driver was healing his head wound while the passenger struggled with the seat belt. Lydia kicked the car, sending it tumbling down the embankment towards the dark field below.

The Cerza on the motorcycle performed a fast slide U-turn and stopped. Sara glanced at her rearview mirror before accelerating away from the scene. The motorcycle driver, his face concealed by his helmet and shaded visor, faced Lydia. The faint pink blotches on his jacket collar marked him as a low-level commander within the Cerza. Relieved that he wasn't following Sara, Lydia glared back at him. He whispered to her.

You're gonna pay for that.

Let's find out, Sarge.

He revved the engines and charged; Lydia heard someone forcing a car door open. She leaped backwards into the night sky.

Below her, the driver stumbled from the vehicle while the passenger remained inside. Lydia landed several feet away and raised her guard. The driver shook his head, then faced Lydia. The driver was a clean-shaven white male who appeared to be in his 40s. He'd healed his wounds, but his shirt was torn. One hole in his shirt revealed part of a Chicago flag tattoo. Lydia made out the words "Serve" and "Protect." The driver snarled at Lydia. Lydia smiled in response.

"Let's role-play," taunted Lydia.

"I'll teach you how," he replied. He rushed at her, but she dodged his first punch.

"Really?" Lydia asked.

Sarge cleared the embankment, then hopped from his motorcycle; the force of his telekinetic push sent him soaring. He prepared to throw a kick as he descended towards Lydia.

For a moment, Lydia felt bemused by Sarge's attempt at a death from above attack. Lydia pivoted away from his aerial kick and countered with her own kick; her strike connected, knocking him out of the air and crashing into the ground.

The driver lunged at her; he threw powerful strikes, most of them failing to connect, while she countered with her own relentless assault. Sarge jumped to his feet and joined the brawl. To Lydia's surprise, they knew how to coordinate their aim. Driver guy targeted her upper body, while Sarge targeted her legs — both trying to hit her at the same time.

Guess they're not total amateurs, she thought.

Lydia backpedaled and circled to keep only one of them before her. Despite her quick strikes and maneuvering, the Cerzas pressed their attack. Her guard absorbed most of the blows, but a few slipped by.

Lydia worried about the passenger joining the assault. Could she hold off three attackers? Her worry faded when she imagined the Cerzas assaulting Sara. Sara wouldn't be able to fight back. Only Lydia could keep them away from her, inflating her rage. She spotted an opening and attacked one of the Sarge's knees; her strike hyper-extended it, and he crumpled to the ground. The driver jumped over the fallen Cerza and threw a kick, which Lydia dodged, countering with a swing of her forearm to his throat. The blow connected and she drove him to the ground. His skull cracked upon impact.

She heard someone behind her, and she spun, leading with her elbow. The passenger ducked and slammed into her side, clinching Lydia, and lifting her from the ground. The passenger smiled as he launched them towards the sky. Lydia struggled to free her arms as he tightened his hold.

"You'll be my first sky—"

Lydia head-butted his face, smashing his nose; she followed it with another headbutt, cracking his jaw. Lydia countered with her own telekinetic push, the sudden jolt surprising the passenger. Lydia took advantage of his surprise and broke his hold; she grabbed him by the hair, shoving two fingers into his eyes. His eyes turned to dust as he screamed.

"Not so tough," said Lydia before she kicked him. The blow sent him plummeting until he crashed into another tree along Briarcliff. The tree shook from the impact as he bounced off it and started tumbling down the embankment.

That should take him out for the night, thought Lydia.

As her ascent slowed, she healed her injuries, taking in the view. The streetlights from Bolingbrook and the other surrounding communities stretched as far as she could see. The cars on I-55 flowed like a river of light.

Decades ago, Matthew, working with anonymous investors, financed the subdivisions that became Bolingbrook. Bolingbrook grew into a community of over 70,000 people. Bolingbrook was Matthew's legacy. It was Sara's home and, tonight, it was her job to protect Bolingbrook from these so-called 'knights'.

Lydia descended. Directly below her, Sarge and the driver waited, each holding a dagger.

I hate knife fights, thought Lydia.

Lydia scanned the field. The motorcycle laid on the ground several yards from her current landing spot. She could see the passenger healing, but his eyes wouldn't finish regenerating tonight.

The fight had been strenuous. Yet Lydia felt confident she could go a few more rounds before needing blood. If it weren't for the weredeer army, Steve would have sent an assault team to deal with the Cerzas. In fact, Steve still could send an assault team. They wouldn't try to kill Aurora or Lydia but dealing with them could be messy. Steve and Matthew didn't need a mess to clean up. She needed to end this.

Lydia fell several yards as the two vampires grinned and raised their knives. Lydia aimed for the motorcycle and pushed. Sarge and the driver watched with their mouths agape as Lydia shot away from them. They didn't know she could recover from telekinetic pushes faster than they could.

"She's full of surprises," Sarge said.

They ran after her.

Lydia touched the ground and used her momentum to roll several feet towards the motorcycle.

"Don't even think about it!" growled Sarge.

Lydia bounced to her feet next to the motorcycle.

"Get away from her!"

Get away from her, thought Lydia. That's what Sheila's father had said. Miriam and Sheila had been taking a break from studying. Miriam asked about baton twirling, and Sheila started teaching her. At some point, they kissed. Did Miriam start it or did Sheila? Did it matter? They blushed afterwards. Both of them liked it, so they returned to kissing. Miriam was excited. She didn't have to hold back anymore. She didn't have to pretend she only liked boys, yet the joy she felt crashed down upon her as soon as Sheila's father charged into the room. He hauled Miriam away from Sheila as hate consumed him.

"Get away from her!"

Miriam thought she'd heard the worst, but she was wrong. Miriam's father picked up where Sheila's father left off. Years of resentment and hate exploded. He always blamed Lydia for ruining his life because her mother died during childbirth. Her perversion, he said, was the last straw. He wished she had never been born and kicked her out of her home. The only home she'd ever known.

Her older sister hung up when she asked for help. Miriam was afraid of what her relatives would say, or how her classmates would treat her. She had to leave and the only person she could run to was in Iowa City — even if he was involved in drug trafficking and other shady businesses. Things only got worse for Miriam. She had to become Lydia to escape, but Lydia couldn't forget who she was. She couldn't forget Miriam's pain.

Sarge's voice brought her back to the present. "I'll dust every limb if you don't get back."

Lydia remained still. The two vampires closed in.

They want to ruin Sara's life, she thought.

"Last chance."

Lydia grabbed the motorcycle and swung it. She knocked Sarge over in a single blow. Then she kicked the driver and smashed the motorcycle over his head. Lydia kept bludgeoning them with the motorcycle. Her attacks savaged both vampires. In her rage, she couldn't tell them apart. They wanted to ruin Sara's life, and that was all that mattered. Lydia kept pounding their ravaged bodies, but she still felt Miriam's pain.

A shotgun blast lit up the field. Lydia stopped attacking as the smell of phosphate hit her. Someone had fired a dragon's breath round. The scout stood by the car wielding two shotguns.

"Don't move." The scout snarled. While his clothes were still torn, he'd fully recovered from the beating Aurora and she had given him. The scout dropped the smoking shotgun and pointed the other at Lydia.

Lydia's thoughts raced. How did he escape? Where's Aurora? Did he harm her? Did someone else harm her? Was it the fifth Cerza?

The scout surveyed the battleground. "I thought you were the good cop." He whistled in astonishment.

Lydia took deep breaths to calm herself.

"Back away!" the scout commanded.

Lydia walked backwards. On the ground, the ravaged vampires moaned. Broken bones poked through their skin. Their faces caved in from her blows. It would be a long time before they could threaten anyone.

Get it together, thought Lydia. You can't afford to fall apart like that again.

The scout advanced past the injured Cerzas. "Stop."

Lydia did.

"Drop the bike."

Lydia locked her eyes on the scout. She considered throwing the motorcycle but rejected the idea. He'd have enough time to dodge it and shoot. She thought she could only use the motorcycle as a weapon if he were distracted.

"I said drop the bike." This time, Lydia sensed the fear in his voice.

Lydia tightened her grip on the ruined motorcycle. She smelled gasoline and noticed oil dripping on her skin. Now the motorcycle was a liability, she thought. His shotgun could ignite the leaking gas and oil. During their sparing sessions, Matthew stressed that if she was conscious, she had options. She tried to think of any other options besides surrendering to a newbie enforcer.

The scout pointed the shotgun at Lydia. "I'll shoot you if I have to. Drop the goddamn bike."

Lydia remembered one of Sheila's performances. Her performances captivated her back then. Lydia's recollection of that performance gave her an idea.

The scout put his finger on the trigger. "Well?"

Lydia started to lower the bike and, as the scout gradually removed his finger from the trigger. Then she heaved the motorcycle towards the sky.

"That works," said the scout. Lydia raised her hands. The scout's eyes lit up with sadistic joy. "That's more like it." He shuddered, then cleared his throat. "As a Rycerz for the Kingdom of Chicago," he said with a hint of fear in his voice. His hands started trembling. "I find you guilty of the following crimes. You housed an invading army, challenged the Dux's rightful claim to Greater Chicago, assaulted officers of the court and mocked the rightful Dux of Chicago." His hands remained trembling as he said, "Speak now before I sentence you."

"Catch."

The motorcycle dropped in front of Lydia, so she spun, hauling her bodyweight to kick it at the scout. The scout pulled the trigger and the motorcycle burst into flames, colliding with him, the impact knocking him to the ground. He screamed as his clothes ignited. The other vampires rolled away as the scout tossed the burning motorcycle off his burning body, screaming and thrashing amongst the flames.

"Roll," ordered Lydia. "Roll on the ground if you don't want to burn to death." The scout started rolling past one of his fellow Cerza and, as he rolled, the flames diminished. Lydia winced when she saw his burns.

All of them will survive, Lydia thought. They can't hurt Sara now.

Lydia heard the faint sound of crumpling leather behind her as she turned. A man in the air kicked her in the chest. As the kick knocked her several feet back; she felt as though a piston had hit her. Lydia lifted her head and let her shoulders absorb the impact, then cursed as she hopped to her feet. The fifth Cerza levitated high in the air: a white male with black hair and a trimmed mustache. Strapped to his back was a dark blue pool cue bag. His clothes bore the Cerza marks, and red marks she'd never seen before. Lydia guessed he was their boss.

The boss dived at Lydia, and she dodged his flying kick. He landed, spinning his body to throw a punch as Lydia leaned back; his fist glanced off her chin and dislocated her jaw. He followed with a kick that fractured her ribs. The boss threw a hard right punch, but Lydia raised her guard as his strike connected, breaking both of her arms. She struggled to maintain her balance. While she knew how to react to getting her bones broken in combat, she still hated the sharp pain, and the sickening sound of breaking bones.

She, however, didn't have experience fighting a much older vampire like the boss. No time like the present, she thought. She kicked the boss, and the blow pushed him backwards. She only had moments before the boss could resume his attack.

Lydia healed her arms and started to backflip, and once the soles of her boots faced the boss, she unleashed her strongest telekinetic push. The force staggered him back as Lydia flew several yards in the opposite direction. Lydia healed her remaining wounds but knew she couldn't keep up the pace.

She landed, using her momentum to perform a back roll and bounce to her feet. The boss hovered over her again, only he wielded a dagger. He dived. Before Lydia could dodge, Aurora swooped in, colliding with the boss midair. They shot by Lydia and crashed into the ground; the dagger fell from his hand. Both recovered quickly, scrambling to their feet. The boss advanced with quick and powerful strikes. Aurora struggled to dodge and block them.

Lydia pulled out her knife and rushed to position herself at the boss' rear flank. If he's focused on Aurora, thought Lydia, I might surprise him. It was a long shot, but better than doing nothing.

Aurora leaped into the air. The boss followed and rocketed up to Aurora; he caught her by the throat, tossing her aimlessly to the ground. Lydia's eyes widened. Aurora impacted the ground face first, moaning as she struggled to push herself back up. The boss landed and picked up his dagger. Lydia charged as the boss pounced on Aurora's back; she swung her knife, just as he plunged his dagger. Lydia's blade intercepted his wrist, severing his hand. The severed hand disintegrated, and the dagger bounced off

Aurora's body. Lydia followed with two strikes of her own, knocking the boss off Aurora, and finishing by thrusting her fingers into his eyes. He screamed and struck Lydia with his knee. The blow knocked Lydia back several feet. The boss levitated. Aurora rolled over as Lydia regained her footing and rushed to her side. Gently, she pulled Aurora to her feet.

Who's that?

Their boss.

The boss landed about five yards in front of Lydia and Aurora; his eyeballs had finished regenerating. Lydia raised her knife while Aurora picked up her own. Raising his right arm, he revealed the stump where his hand had been. Bones sprouted from the stump, making a crackling sound as they grew. Lydia had never seen someone regenerate a limb that fast. Even Matthew needed a day to regrow a finger.

"Lydia?" Aurora, her voice trembling, backed away from the boss. But Lydia maintained her knife fighting stance.

You don't really know Sara.

Lydia waited.

Do you really want to risk everything for her?

Soft flesh creeped up the boss' new bones.

Is she worth it?

"My name is Lydia and I represent the Vitalis Corporation."

His skin started regenerating.

"You are trespassing on Vitalis property. Your Dux has no legitimate claim to Bolingbrook or its residents."

The boss focused on Lydia. He'd healed his other wounds and would be fully recovered once his hand regenerated.

"We're not allied with the weredeer. We do not believe they are a threat to your kingdom. If we need your help, we will ask for it. Until then. Get the *hell* out of Bolingbrook!"

The boss' right hand finished regenerating. He looked down at Lydia and Aurora with his cold, calculating gaze. It was as if he regarded them as annoyances, rather than opponents. Aurora reluctantly assumed a fighting stance as she looked up in fear at the boss.

"Final warning," said Lydia, undaunted by the deadly predator hovering above her.

He unsnapped the top of the bag strapped to his back and began to draw his sword.

Oh shit! Lydia?

Yet the boss stopped and looked up.

Several hundred feet above them, shadows fluttered around a humanoid figure, like a sheet of fabric. Lydia struggled to peer through the shadows, only able to make out a person who presented as female. Few vampires could blend into the shadows like that.

Aurora whispered, *Is that The Counselor?*

Lydia nodded. She'd heard the rumor that the Counselor was one of the original 11 vampires. Judging by the boss's reaction, and her shadow blending skills, Lydia believed it.

Aurora whispered. *I don't know if I should be grateful or worried.*

We'll find out.

The boss closed the bag and turned away from the Counselor. The scout limped past him; he had healed his face, but he was still bald. Burns covered his hands and legs.

"The Dux's High Counselor apologizes for the—" The scout looked up at the Counselor. He seemed surprised. He blinked several times, and, after a few moments, he looked back at Aurora and Lydia. "She apologizes for this misunderstanding. She will remind all Rycerz of the Vitalis Corporation's legitimate claim to Bolingbrook. We will leave your territory at once. The Counselor does request that you forward any information about the weredeer that may be of use to us." He closed his eyes, then spoke slowly as if reading a script. "The weredeer invaders are a threat to the Kingdom and the free territories. So, the Kingdom will send a delegation to... establish diplomatic relations." The scout sighed. "You'd better accept her generous offer." He added, sounding more like himself.

A gray SUV parked on Briarcliff and the Cerzas hobbled towards it, while the boss flew towards Chicago. The Counselor faded into the night sky.

Lydia and Aurora waited in silence for several moments. The motorcycle's flames were dimming. Divots and craters littered the field. The wrecked car's lights had flickered out during the battle.

Aurora broke the silence first. "You know, the only reason I helped you is because Matthew would have killed me if you died."

Lydia shrugged.

"Do you really want to bring Sara into our world?"

***

Lydia had been in many dangerous situations. Yet she had never felt this afraid as she walked towards the *Babbler's* offices. She had to try; Lydia told herself. She couldn't go on like this. Steve's rejection last night hurt, but it also meant she could move on. Find another person to understand her. Someone who could end her loneliness. Lydia and Aurora planned to leave the next night. It could be years before she returned.

Babbler staffers began streaming out of the office, and Lydia felt her heart tense. She blended with the shadows and jumped onto the roof of the neighboring auto repair shop, chiding her panic, and felt fortunate that Aurora was searching for the surviving Reds.

Lydia didn't see Sara's car when she arrived. Had something happened to her? Lydia scanned the entire parking lot. Did she park somewhere else? Was she captured? Was she dead? Or worse?

"They're positive it's Tom?" asked Sara.

Lydia pivoted as Sara and Wendy stepped outside. Wendy was a white female, who was taller than Sara and appeared to be in her fifties. She wore a purple blouse and a black skirt. Sara wore a blue blouse.

"Absolutely," Wendy replied. "The crew took him straight to Clow. He was driving the second car when that weredeer ran onto Boughton."

Lydia stepped off the roof and pushed to slow her fall, landing in a shaded area. She could walk towards Sara once Wendy left.

"This complicates matters," Sara said.

"Possibly," Wendy replied. "But Reese won't let them scramble Tom's brain. He'll try to recruit Tom. Then Robert might decide to make a counteroffer."

Sara nodded thoughtfully. "It would be a shame if he accepted either."

"I agree. He'd make a talented reporter, and it would be nice to have one more ex-skeptic on staff."

"It would be. For now, we can only wait."

Lydia took a few tentative steps forward. Did she risk introducing herself with Wendy watching? Sara's phone vibrated. She pulled it out and looked at the screen. "Can Don and you lock up?"

Wendy hesitated before answering, "I guess."

"Are you sure?"

Wendy paused, then relaxed with a smile. "Yes. It's his last night, so I can do it. If he doesn't bring up his illegal alien abduction theory, I won't bring up my temporal rift theory."

"See you tomorrow, then."

Wendy stepped back inside as Sara looked out at Boughton Road before putting her phone away.

Lydia walked to the edge of the shade. Another step and Sara could see her. Thoughts flooded her mind. Was she wearing the wrong outfit? Was her skin too pale? What if Sara knew about Steve? Would Sara get the wrong idea? Did Sara even like women?

Just try, thought Lydia. Just try.

Lydia stepped out of the shadows and approached Sara, just as a car drove into the lot and parked by Sara. Lydia halted as an African American male stepped out. He was clean shaven and wore a polo-shirt with black slacks. "Hey," he said.

Sara grinned. "Hi, honey."

They embraced each other, lost in a kiss.

Lydia froze, a pit in her stomach; when they released their embrace; she noticed their wedding bands. Their embrace reminded Lydia of the love-struck college students she'd see around Iowa City. Sara and her husband had the same passion for each other as those students had. Sometimes Lydia felt jealous and sad because she believed that kind of relationship wasn't possible for her. As she watched Sara and her husband, those feelings and doubts returned.

Lydia asked herself why she didn't notice Sara's wedding band. Was she too distracted?

"Dinner is on me tonight," said the man.

"What about—"

"Monique and Jacob are with my parents."

Sara's eyes lit up as she grinned. "Ooh. We haven't had a date night in ages."

Lydia stepped behind a tree and blended into the shadows.

Sara's husband smiled back at Sara. "That's why we're going to Los Lisle."

"Wow!" said Sara. "We haven't been there since our very first date."

"Which means it's been too long since we've been there."

Sara chuckled. "Peter, sometimes you surprise me."

Peter and Sara entered the car. Lydia stepped out of the shadows as Peter backed out of the parking spot. She wondered if she should wave or do something to let Sara know she existed. The car drove away, and Lydia trembled as she watched them leave. She imagined Sara with her children, picturing her smiling at each of them like the way she smiled at Peter. She imagined what their children looked like. Each one had to be as beautiful and loving as Sara. Lydia's legs wobbled, and she dropped to her knees.

All I did for her, thought Lydia. All I risked for her. For nothing. It's not fair. Aurora was right.

Lydia's eyes struggled to produce tears, so she covered her face and heard herself sob.

Stop it, Lydia thought. Stop being selfish like Aurora and the others.

Lydia breathed and rocked back and forth to calm herself.

Lydia answered herself. But it hurts. It hurts being alone. I don't want to be alone; I don't want to be like Aurora.

Her eyes stopped trying to cry, but her hands still covered her face. In her mind, she replayed Sara and Peter's kiss over and over. Each of Peter's kisses and hugs stung as she recalled them.

Lydia recalled Sara's smile and the way she hugged Peter. The way Sara's face seemed to glow in his presence. The sparkle in her brown eyes. Sara was happy. Lydia's mood changed, as if she was feeling Sara's happiness, too.

Isn't that enough? She wondered. Lydia uncovered her face but kept her eyes closed.

You care about Sara, she told herself. Remember how happy she was? Think about it. The woman you care about is happy.

Lydia pictured Sara and Peter with their children.

You saved Sara, she told herself. You saved her family.

Lydia imagined the Chicago Kingdom sending more vampires after Sara. If she left, who would protect them? Should she stay in Bolingbrook? How would Matthew react? Would he disown her, or worse?

You can't stay. The panicked thoughts stopped. You still need your family. Steve promised to protect the residents of Bolingbrook. Remember? Sara's a resident. Steve can protect her. He has the resources to protect her.

Lydia opened her eyes. She looked up at the door to the newsroom. She started imagining the weredeer, hunters, and other vampires attacking Sara. Could Steve stop all of them?

Stop it, she told herself. Even if she died, you still gave her more time with her family. More time with her friends. More time in the job she loves. You can't always protect her. Could you stand watching her every night with Peter? It would be too painful. What if she caught you spying on her?

She heard footsteps coming from inside the newsroom. Lydia's body felt too weighed down to move. No one at the *Babbler* knew who or what she was. If anyone noticed her, they'd think she was a heartbroken twenty-something. Why would they care? Why would anyone care about her?

That's not the point, she told herself. Think of what you did for her. Sara won't be haunted by traumatic memories. Let that be your gift to her, even if she'll never know what you did. You'll always know. That's enough. Don't be like the other vampires. Be different. Even if it makes you lonely. Be better than them!

The door opened, and Wendy and Don stepped out. Don still didn't know how to iron his shirts, Lydia thought.

"Ma'am?" Don asked. "Are you okay?"

Lydia considered the question. She nodded and stood up.

Wendy said, "We could call a cab or a—"

"No," Lydia smiled. "I'm fine. I'm much better now."

"If you say so," said Don.

Lydia turned and walked away, looking up into the night. The stars in the sky calmed her.

Maybe I'm on the right track, thought Lydia. Maybe there is someone who can love me as much as I love them. Someone I don't have to keep secrets from. Someone I can bring into my world.

The End

***

The next book is The Rift. *Find out what happens next to Sara, Tom, Wendy, and the weredeer army.*

If you want to learn about the choices Miriam/Lydia and Sara made that brought them into Bolingbrook's shadows, their stories are in Pathways to Bolingbrook.

Lydia will return.

Thank You

Thank you for reading this book. Please consider leaving a review at Goodreads and/or where you got a copy. Even a single-sentence review could encourage someone to get a copy.

For updates about my writing and bonus content, you can subscribe to my mailing list using the link below:

Mailing List: https://bolingbrookbabbler.com/mailing-list

Acknowledgments

It took a team to bring *A Fire in the Shadows* to fruition.

Thanks to my wife for her love and support over the years. We've been on quite a journey.

Thanks to my editor for her help in getting this manuscript in shape.

Thanks to my newsletter subscribers for helping me to select the title. If you want to subscribe, go to www .bolingbrookbabbler.com.

Thanks to my fellow bloggers at *Freethought Blogs*. I'm still learning from them after all these years.

Thanks to the independent authors who have helped me over the years. A rising tide lifts all boats.

Thank you for taking the time to read this book.

Finally, I'd like to mention two groups that help LGBTQ+ young people. The first is the Trevor Project, which provides trained counseling services to LGBTQ+ youth 24/7. You can learn more about them at https:/ /www.thetrevorproject.org. The second group is Bolingbrook Pride. They support the LGBTQ+ community in Bolingbrook and the surrounding suburbs. Please go to https://www.bolingbrookpride.org to learn more about them, and consider making a donation.

About William Brinkman

In William Brinkman's world, suburban sidewalks lead to secret conspiracies, emotional reckonings, and the occasional enraged weredeer. He writes urban fantasy with a blend of satire and heart, offering humanistic views of the real world through a supernatural lens. Since 1999, he's published the Bolingbrook Babbler blog, which inspired—but remains separate from—his fiction. His book, *A Fire in the Shadows*, made the short list for the 2024 Indieverse Award for Best Novella. A former Bolingbrook resident, William now lives in suburban Chicagoland with his wife and two cats.

For updates and a free eBook, *God to Smite Bolingbrook*, sign up for his newsletter.

https://bolingbrookbabbler.com/mailing-list

g

goodreads.com/author/show/5699299.William_Brinkman

f

facebook.com/bolingbrookbabbler/

♪

tiktok.com/@williambrinkmanbb

THE RIFT

A BOLINGBROOK BABBLER STORY
BOOK 2

WILLIAM BRINKMAN

Preview of The Rift

Tom Larsen had everything a skeptic blogger could want: loyal followers, a steady stream of income, and multiple outlets. To the skeptic community, he's one of the brave heroes defending the movement against a takeover attempt by "radical feminists" like podcaster Jamie Kyle. But deep down inside, Tom is still fuming over a video Jamie posted about him.

When Tom finds out that Jamie and the other feminist skeptics are going to hold a congress in his hometown of Bolingbrook, he sees a chance to get his revenge. He just needs one media outlet to let him cover the Congress.

Unfortunately, the only media organization willing to meet with him is the *Bolingbrook Babbler*. Tom's hometown tabloid is infamous for its sensational articles about an alien base under Bolingbrook, and cryptids roaming the neighboring forest preserves. The *Babbler* is the anthesis of everything the skeptical movement stands for. But desperate times call for desperate measures...

The Rift: Chapter 3

"*The mission of skeptical organizations is to promote skepticism. Anything else is mission drift.*"
—@thativancabot

AS TOM APPROACHED THE strip malls along Barber's Corner in his blue Toyota Echo, he could make out the words *Bolingbrook Babbler* among the red brick buildings. The gray concrete slab roofs brought World War II bunkers to mind. Across Route 53, he could see the new Portillo's building and the businesses that replaced the East Boughton Drive Jewel-Osco store where his parents used to shop.

Tom made a left turn on the access road. After a short drive, he turned into the parking lot and soon found himself in front of the *Babbler's* office. Two days ago, he never would have imagined himself here.

After the board meeting, still high from his public comments, Tom had approached the village clerk, thinking she would give him a form to fill out to become a registered Bolingbrook media outlet. Instead, she recorded his information and said she had a backlog of applications to approve. Tom suspected she wasn't telling him the truth. She suggested Tom ask one of the registered outlets to sponsor him. Otherwise, he could be waiting at least a month.

The drive home had been one of the worst car trips he'd taken with his parents since they went to Malta, Illinois and got lost in the corn maze. This time his parents ceaselessly grilled him on his remarks. When they offered to pay for him to see a therapist, Tom refused. As his parents kept insisting he needed help, Tom wondered why his mother, whom he considered a rational feminist, didn't understand.

The next day had only made matters worse. He emailed all the suburban newspapers, asking if any were interested in a story about the Humanist Heart congress. As a joke, he even emailed a pitch to the *Babbler*, penning a fake story in their style. He remembered laughing as he emailed them. Surely, he thought, at least one serious news outlet would accept his pitch. How could they not cover a feminist invasion of suburbia?

None of the area papers were interested—one editor even offered to pray for him. Well, almost none. The editor of the *Babbler* had been interested, and insisted on meeting in person.

Tom stood at the front door. Painted on the glass were the words: *Bolingbrook's first and only true tabloid since 1965.* Tom let out a sigh and trudged in.

Entering a room of brown cubicles, Tom heard some members of staff talking on the phone, while others typed away at their keyboards. A front counter and two side counters separated the reception area from the newsroom. Framed copies of old *Babbler* issues lined the walls. To his far left, he saw a door and made out the word "Publisher." *Probably the only actual office in this building.*

Tom noticed a woman at an open-air desk. She was wearing a gray textured t-shirt and faded jeans. Tom thought she looked familiar, but couldn't recall why.

The woman looked up from her computer. "Can I help you?"

"I have a meeting with Sara," Tom replied.

"You must be Tom." She stood up and walked towards the counter. "I'm Wendy Onofrey. Pleased to meet you." Tom shook her hand. "Sara got called into a meeting with our publisher. Something about a job applicant." Wendy lifted the hinged part of the counter and opened a small door. "You can wait back here with me."

As Tom walked into the news area, Wendy motioned for him to sit in a chair by her desk.

"You wouldn't happen to be that job applicant?"

Tom shook his head. "Just submitting a piece. If it goes well, maybe she'll let me cover a special event at the Golf Club."

"Humanist Heart?"

Tom raised his eyebrows. "You've heard of them?"

"Of course," Wendy replied. "It's our job to know what's going on in Bolingbrook."

Tom fought the urge to make a snarky remark as he sat down. "I hope she'll let me cover it."

Wendy nodded. "If you do, investigate why they're holding it here. The Golf Club doesn't exactly scream social justice. Plus, Robert doesn't strike me as one of them. Though I think the official story is right about one thing: It would be the safest place. It is the secondary command center for Bolingbrook."

"Oh. I think I remember reading about that."

"A reader," Wendy replied. "I like that."

"Well—"

"Lots of residents just glance at our covers. I like the ones who take the time to read our articles."

Tom politely nodded, wondering when Sara's meeting would end.

Wendy continued. "Anyway. It'll be interesting to see what happens. Like I said, it's the safest place in Illinois, next to Clow Base, of course. Considering they found a bomb at the last location, they'll need the protection."

Tom chuckled. "I guess the village will protect them while they conspire against the skeptical movement."

Wendy shook her head. "Actually, that's not the point of this meeting. From what I've read, they're divided between the forum-only faction and the non-profit faction. So, this is really a congress about the future of the group. Do they stick with being an Internet space for progressive skeptics, or do they become a progressive version of the Habenstein Society? They also need to decide if they want to work with other groups. Since some of them will have observers there, it should be a lively event."

"I expect it will be. All the drama should interest your readers."

Wendy looked closer at Tom, then raised her finger. "Say, did you used to write a blog?"

"Still do. It's called *Skeptical Hurricane*."

"Oh." Wendy looked uncomfortable as she leaned away. "I remember when it was *Skeptical Butterfly*."

Tom failed to contain his surprise.

"Back when I posted on the Habenstein Society's forums," said Wendy, "I remember seeing a lot of links to your posts. I enjoyed reading them."

Tom furrowed his brow. "You used to be a skeptic?"

"Still am."

"You are?" Tom stumbled. "I didn't expect..."

"To find a skeptic here? Actually, this is the best place for a skeptic. I've learned more here than I ever did in the skeptical movement."

"You left the movement?"

"It left me."

"Onofrey? Are you related—"

"To the guy who trolls skeptics? Yes. We used to be identical."

"Oh," Tom replied.

The back door opened. A man and woman walked in, carrying bags and drinks from Portillo's.

"Lunchtime!" said the woman, who wore a black pantsuit and appeared to be close to Tom's age. Tom admired her copper hair for a moment, then turned his attention back to Wendy.

"Perfect," Wendy replied, then looked at Tom. "Portillo's day is one of the few perks we have."

Other staff members emerged from the cubicles. While the man placed most of the bags on a table, the woman approached with a bag marked for Wendy. Wendy accepted it, and the woman glanced at the publisher's office.

"They're still meeting?"

"Yep," Wendy replied. "I think he wasn't too pleased. Especially if he called Sara in."

The woman stared at the door for a few moments, then faced Wendy. "They should be done soon. Oh, your friend says thanks for lunch. He's seen two rifts this week."

"Thanks. I'll take care of it."

"Sure." The woman noticed Tom and stepped closer. "Have we met?"

"I don't think so."

"Excuse me," said Wendy. "I forgot my manners. Tom, this is Jenna Olson, our sales representative, and one of our resident psychics."

Jenna smiled. "Actually, I prefer the term percipient."

"Jenna," Wendy continued, "This is Tom. He wants to submit a piece."

"Oh!" said Jenna. "So, what's your article about?"

"You're asking?" said Tom.

"Yes?" Jenna replied.

"You're the psychic." Tom closed his eyes and imagined the answer. When he opened them, he saw Jenna frowning at him.

"That was rude," she said. "You shouldn't test someone without asking. And if you're going to, do the right test, because I have precognition, not telepathy."

"My apologies," Tom sarcastically replied. "I don't normally hang out with precogs."

"Don't mention that movie."

"Noted. So, what am I doing next week?"

Jenna glared at Tom for a moment, then her face relaxed. She tilted her head, then stepped closer, squinting her eyes for a few moments before straightening her posture and stepping back.

"That's odd," she said. "It seems like you're not doing anything next week."

"Nothing?"

"Nothing. Wait." She tilted her head again. "Something about you feels off."

"Off?" Tom asked. "Ah. I get it. You just need my credit card number to fine tune your vision."

"No," Jenna snapped.

"Something *is* wrong," added Wendy. "She should see something, even if you're dead next week."

"Yet I don't see or sense anything about you," said Jenna. "You're full of surprises, Tom."

"I suppose," Tom answered. "Or maybe you know better than to try a cold reading—"

"Really?" Jenna replied, frowning.

"She isn't a cold reader," said Wendy. "Notice she didn't flood you with questions."

"But she gave a vague answer."

"I was very specific," protested Jenna.

"'Nothing' is a specific answer?"

"Yes."

"So I'm going to cease to exist next week?"

Wendy shook her head. "More likely her brain can't process what she's seeing."

"Process?"

"Let me show you." Wendy picked up a business card and wrote Tom's name, placed the card in her hand, then turned both her palms down on the desk. "Where's the card?"

"Your other hand?"

Wendy showed Tom both of her empty palms. "Our brains make mistakes." She pulled the card out of her desk drawer and placed it in front of Tom. He saw his name written on it. "Our brains are evolved to make assumptions, and some of those assumptions are wrong—you were fooled by my misdirection. Jenna sees parts of the future, but can't always tell what she's looking at."

Tom reluctantly nodded.

"Reese taught me that trick," said Wendy. "If you want to be published in the *Babbler*, you really should be more open-minded."

Tom felt his face warm with embarrassment. He still didn't believe Jenna was a psychic, but he needed access to the congress.

"While I have questions," Tom sighed. "I'm sorry you were hurt by how I asked them."

"You're sorry I was offended?" asked Jenna.

"Yes," said Tom. He decided humor might lighten things. "I'm sorry, and I promise to never introduce you to Anti-Psychic Kitty."

"Tom," said Wendy. "Anti-Psychic Kitty almost killed her father."

"Seriously? The CAS's mascot? How?"

"That is a *very* long story," came a new voice. Tom turned and saw a Black woman in her late thirties wearing a white blouse with gray slacks. "Which my staff don't have time to tell because we have *an issue. To finish.*"

Tom stood up. "I'm—"

"I know who you are. Sara Langston, editor. We have a lot to talk about." She offered her hand, shaking Tom's firmly, then motioned for him to follow.

Jenna approached Tom. "Before you go, there's one thing I should tell you. Bolingbrook is known as the Pathway Village. Don't be afraid to change paths."

Jenna smiled before returning to Wendy's desk.

Tom gave Jenna a puzzled look, then followed Sara into her cubicle. The divider walls were bare, but behind the desk was a small bookshelf. On top of it were pictures he assumed were of her husband and daughter. Two books stood out to Tom: a worn copy of a guide to haunted places in Chicago, and one titled *Blood in the Wind: The Secret History of Chicagoland's Vampire Kingdoms and Free Territories.*

Sara motioned towards the chair in front of her desk. Tom sat and placed a printout of his article in front of her. For the first time since college, an editor was about to review his writing. Sara sat down, clicked her wireless mouse, and turned her attention to her screen. Tom removed a pen from his shirt pocket and set it next to the printout.

"You aren't making my job easy," said Sara.

"Oh?"

"Our publisher has concerns about printing anything by you. Insulting his granddaughter didn't help your case."

Tom suddenly felt like he'd swallowed a black hole. The Olson family owned the *Babbler*. He should have recognized Jenna's last name.

"Oh God," Tom heard himself whisper. "I can apologize right now. It's just—um. I'm sorry. It won't happen again."

"Good," Sara replied. "Considering Jenna's visions are one reason I invited you here, I hope you'll show her more respect."

"I will," Tom blurted out.

"That's good to hear. You can take a minute."

"Thank you," said Tom as he tried to calm himself down. After a few deep breaths, he relaxed. "I'm ready."

"Good. So, let's start with your sample story."

Tom felt his confidence return. "You're welcome to publish it, and if you need any minor corrections—"

"You made this up."

Tom waited several uncomfortable moments for Sara to continue. She continued to glare at him.

Say something.

"And?" asked Tom.

Sara leaned towards him. "You wrote a piece of fiction. A sloppy piece of fiction. We don't print fiction here."

Tom's jaw dropped. *How can I be blowing this?*

"Look at your story," said Sara. "It's about Gray-type aliens. There's no such thing as Grays. Then you brought Bigfoot into it. Bolingbrook doesn't have a Bigfoot population. Even if it did, aliens don't carry away Bigfoot corpses. They turn to dust. I also know you didn't interview any aliens. That's just the first paragraph." Tom gulped as Sara continued. "I could go on, but let me get to the point: We're not a literary magazine and we don't print fiction."

"Come on," Tom protested. "If I'm guilty of anything, it's not paying close attention to your recent stories. I'll read some more—"

"I said we don't publish fiction."

"But everyone in Bolingbrook knows your stories aren't real. *I* know they're not real. I grew up here. I've seen Hidden Lakes. I've walked the trails. We laugh at your articles because we know they're not real. You can't criticize me because my story is fiction when everything the *Babbler*'s ever published is fictional. And that's beside the point—I want to write about something real!"

Sara shook her head. "Maybe if I'd spent as many years among skeptics as you, I wouldn't think twice about submitting this. Maybe I'd feel like pranking the *Babbler* was serving humanity. But let me assure you, Tom. All the articles we publish are about something real."

Tom blinked. "Are you seriously trying to tell me you believe everything you publish?"

Sara leaned back in her chair and paused for a moment. "Of course I do. My name is on the masthead. Before I worked here, I thought the stories were fiction. But let's just say after I had a run-in with the men in blue, I became more open-minded. That nearly got me fired from my previous paper, but I wanted to know the truth. So, I feel very fortunate to work for the *Babbler*. Our content may seem like a joke to you, but we make sure we thoroughly research stories before publishing them. Do you believe me now?"

Tom considered the possibilities. "I... understand that you believe what you publish."

"That's a good start."

Time to recover.

"So, I apologize for writing a fiction piece. I didn't know how committed you and your staff are to reporting what you believe is the truth. I hope I can make up for it by writing a story—a real story—for you. Let me tell you what I have to offer."

"I'm listening," said Sara.

"Let's start with my YouTube channel."

"Let's not."

Tom swallowed.

Sara continued. "Let's talk about your blog. Back when it was *Skeptical Butterfly*, you did a good job. You were more thorough than most skeptics, even though you toed the party line. Then once your pass at Jamie Kyle backfired, you—"

"*You!*" Tom looked closer at Sara. His eyes widened. "You were at our table that night."

"I was. When I saw Jamie's video, it was obvious who she was talking about."

"You told my editor."

"Yes, but it wasn't my goal to get you fired. I wanted her to give you a warning. Our publisher, however, either feared a lawsuit or wanted an excuse to let you go. Were you aware of the layoffs that followed your release?"

Tom stood up and turned.

"I can get you into the Golf Club."

Tom stopped as desperation overpowered his anger. He turned and faced Sara, who was still sitting at her desk.

"I'm working on securing a press pass for the congress. If we don't get one, we have the connections necessary to get someone in undercover. Wendy has the background to cover the congress, but she's responsible for the layout and the website. I can't risk putting her out in the field."

"I see your point."

Sara continued. "I've looked at the stories you wrote in college. You were an excellent investigative journalist. That article on corruption in UIC's student government? Impressive."

"Thank you?" Tom replied, hesitant.

"Not every reporter can say they forced a politician to leave the country. You know where he is now?"

"I heard he's running a casino for the Russian mob."

"That's my understanding. It takes courage to do investigative journalism."

"I guess," Tom replied.

"But I have a question. Your blog says you're a man going your own way. Correct?"

"Basically."

"So why not keep going? You have a successful blog and podcast with thousands of followers. You're a leader in your movement, even if you don't think of yourself as one. Why do you have to go to this meeting? I won't send you there if you're just going to harass Jamie."

Tom's heart sped up again. "I'm not! This is—"

"Good. Sit down."

Tom sat down.

"What do you know about weredeer?"

***

Tom sighed as he drove east. It was after 11 PM, and to the north, he could just make out the old landfill mound—Mount Bolingbrook, as he liked to call it. To the south, he could see the fence securing the Elmhurst-Chicago quarry. *Another uneventful night.*

He'd read about weredeer in the *Babbler,* and unfortunately still remembered key details. They were like werewolves, except their animal phenotype was a deer. They could shift into one of three forms: humanoid, deer, and alpha. As Sara had reminded him, a weredeer in its alpha form could hold its own in a fight with a dire wolf. She had also reminded him they couldn't mate with each other. While they could mate with normal deer, some weredeer obsessively focused on mating with humans.

Sara had also claimed that there were two local factions of weredeer: suburban and feral. In the 1990s, the suburban weredeer, persuaded by the Bolingbrook Jaycees, agreed to abide by traditional human courtship customs, even if it reduced the chance of producing weredeer born from humans. In exchange, the village would recognize them as Bolingbrook residents. A minority rejected the deal. Not wanting to be hunted by the village's Department of Paranormal Affairs, the feral weredeer retreated to the forest preserves, pledging only to mate with deer.

As a teenager, Tom remembered laughing at the *Babbler's* blurry photos of weredeer in their alpha form. If anyone showed him a blurry photo of Bigfoot, Tom would counter by showing them a blurry photo of a weredeer. Why, Tom would ask, did people believe in Bigfoot but not weredeer, despite there being more photographic evidence for the latter? Some of his classmates told him he was an asshole, while others just called him Bolingbrook High's official class skeptic.

Now the class skeptic was driving down Royce Road trying to find a creature that only existed on the pages of the *Babbler*. According to Sara, hundreds of feral weredeer from around the country were gathering for unknown reasons in the nearby woods. His assignment was to investigate.

This was how Tom had spent most of the week. He'd interviewed all the people on Sara's list of weredeer eyewitnesses. Most sounded sincere, but no one had caught an unambiguous view of a weredeer. A few claimed to have seen something in the woods that moved too fast to be a normal deer. One witness said she'd been walking towards Hidden Lakes Historic Trout Farm and "heard a foreign-sounding voice." Then, she said, a deer had jumped out of the woods, and "glared" at her.

The field skepticism workshops at Habencon portrayed fieldwork as informative, exciting, and short. Old Man Jake from the Committee for Humanism and Skepticism had bragged about all the new skills he'd learned from his investigations, like how to break a board with his hands. The "ghost couple" from France had claimed they could debunk any haunted site in a single night. The Open Investigations Team had countless funny videos debunking psychics. Tom wasn't learning anything, he wasn't having fun, and wasn't even close to resolving the "weredeer mystery." Exhausted and frustrated, he took comfort in knowing that he only had one more area to check out before he could go to bed. Fortunately, it was close to his apartment.

From his phone, which was plugged into the Echo's stereo, Trevor DeBruin's voice jolted Tom back to the present. "It is time to put away the beliefs that now drive feminism," he said. "Time for a philosophy that celebrates sexuality instead of shaming men. Time for a society that does not favor females. If saying so makes us bigots in the eyes of the headless humanists, then so be it. We know the truth." Tom smiled as he reached the intersection of Royce and Route 53.

How many times would he have to investigate weredeer sightings before Wendy and Sara believed they weren't real? It was amazing how the *Babbler's* staff were so committed to its worldview. How could Wendy believe it as well? Having read the same books and followed the same blogs as Tom, even attended conventions years before him, how could she possibly believe in the paranormal?

When Tom reached the intersection of North Ashbury and Boughton, he turned right. Despite his boredom, Tom intently scanned the neighborhood as he drove south. The houses were a mix of brick ranch homes and two-story houses with white vinyl siding. Evenly spaced adolescent trees lined the parkway. If there were deer or weredeer in the area, they weren't in anyone's yards. Tom suspected that in thirty to fifty years, the street would look like it had a green canopy. His friends from Chicago complained that neighborhoods like these made Bolingbrook feel cookie-cutter, but driving through these subdivisions made Tom feel like he was home.

A few minutes later, movement to the right caught Tom's attention. He slowed down and turned the car slightly so its headlights would illuminate the scene. Ahead, he recognized a white-tailed stag with four points on each antler. The buck, its back turned towards Tom, had its front legs perched on a windowsill. It looked strong, like one of the many airbrushed deer photos he saw in magazines and on hunting websites. Right now, it appeared to be sniffing the window. Tom opened the glove compartment, pulling out his flashlight after a few seconds of fumbling and flicking it on. To his relief, the light came on.

Tom drove several feet forward; the deer was now directly to his right. He pointed the flashlight at the buck, which dropped from the window and turned to face him. Tom shone the light at its face. The deer's eyes reflected the white glare, and Tom cursed himself for even entertaining the thought that this was more than a very curious deer. Tom turned off the flashlight, but instead of vanishing, the glow in the creature's eyes turned to electric blue.

Tom's muscles tensed, his eyelids peeling back as if by force, and his right foot instinctively slammed on the accelerator. The Echo's engine roared to life as it sped away from the beast. Tom dropped the flashlight and clenched the steering wheel, hands trembling. In the rearview mirror, he saw the deer's fiery eyes.

Instinctively, Tom turned left onto Independence Lane, tires barely gripping the road. Soon, the houses obscured his view of the deer. After two blocks, Tom slammed on the brakes and struggled to catch his breath, heart still racing. Tom noticed Trevor's video still playing on his phone.

"I'm going to be joining protesters at Humanist Heart International's congress," came Trevor's voice. Tom smiled and relaxed, reaching down to recover his phone from the floor. "As my long-time followers know, I'm going, even if the area isn't wheelchair accessible. What about the rest of you sitting on the fence? I'm sure most of you have two working legs. What's your excuse?"

Tom placed his phone in the passenger seat and looked up. In the rearview mirror, Tom glimpsed a large dark shape descending from the sky. A moment later, it landed on top of a parked car with a loud crash. The landing crushed the roof of the car, setting off its alarm. Tom closed his eyes and shook his head, then turned to look through the rear window.

What looked like an alpha deer stood on top of the car, pummeling the hood. Each punch dented the metal like a jackhammer. If it was an alpha, the photos Tom had seen didn't convey their actual size. The points of its antlers looked razor sharp, its front legs now resembling a gorilla's arms, hind legs sporting talons instead of hooves. It stopped punching and opened its hands, revealing clawed fingers that glistened in the streetlights. The creature swiped at the car's hood, shredding it like cardboard and tossing it away. The hood swam through the air before crashing through a neighboring home's windows.

The weredeer looked towards Tom's car, its eyes still fiery blue. It roared in Tom's direction, revealing a set of shark-like teeth while shaking the Echo.

Tom slammed on the accelerator. The car struggled to pick up speed, while the creature charged on its hands and feet, biting down seconds later into the car's trunk. Over

Trevor's voice, Tom could hear the steel being ripped off. In the mirror, he saw the creature with a sizable chunk of blue metal in its mouth. It slowed down as it chewed.

Tom shifted the car into fifth, continuing to gather speed. He sped past the stop sign as the road merged with North Ashbury. Behind him, the creature spit out the remaining scraps of metal and resumed its pursuit. All the other side streets in this direction were dead ends, Tom remembered: his only hope of escape was to get back to Boughton. The Echo was now up to highway speed and the weredeer was still gaining. Tom pressed the accelerator against the floor. *It has to break off at some point.*

The Echo's tires squealed as the road curved, and the weredeer slowed slightly as it made the turn, then resumed closing in. As the road meandered, the Echo barely held onto the pavement, while the weredeer cut the distance by moving straight. Boughton was now visible and only seconds away. Though the traffic was light, he knew making a left turn at this speed would be impossible. The weredeer was only inches behind.

Tom spun the steering wheel, desperately attempting a hard right onto Boughton. As he heard a car horn blaring at him, he closed his eyes. Instead of a collision, he heard the approaching car crash into the weredeer. Before the outside world tilted, Tom opened his eyes and glimpsed the creature tumbling to the ground in the rearview mirror.

What happens next? Get The Rift: A Bolingbrook Babbler Story *to find out.*

Also By William Brinkman

The Bolingbrook Babbler Stories

- *Pathways to Bolingbrook: A Bolingbrook Babbler Story* Book 1(2021)

- *A Fire in the Shadows: A Bolingbrook Babbler Story Book 1.5 (2023)*

- *The Rift: A Bolingbrook Babbler Story* Book 2 (2022)

- *Revenge of the Phantom Press: A Bolingbrook Babbler Story* Book 3 (2026)

Web Fiction Collection

- God to Smite Bolingbrook (2023)

Demon: The Fallen (White Wolf Studios)

- *Demon: The Fallen* (2002)

- *Saviors and Destroyers* "Broken Bonds" (2003)

- *Damned and Deceived* "The Good Soldier"

(2003)

www.ingramcontent.com/pod-product-compliance
Lightning Source LLC
Chambersburg PA
CBHW050905180626
46814CB00007B/2906

* 9 7 9 8 9 8 5 5 3 7 0 5 5 *